In a hidden corner of faraway

Tasmania,

three Tasmanian devil pups waited.

# Little Devils

## Robert J. Blake

Philomel Books • Penguin Young Readers Group

Burnie and Winnie and Big Stanley could hardly wait for their mum to return to the den.

Sometimes she brought back a fish to eat. Sometimes she brought back a bone to chew on. And sometimes she brought back things that she had borrowed from a nearby fishing cabin—things like a dented frying pan, a footy ball, or an old boot.

Mum didn't mind when the pups wrestled over something that she brought home. She didn't mind when they growled and tore the thing apart. She didn't even mind when Big Stanley lowered his head, said, "Orph," and bashed the thing away from his mates.

Because that is what Tasmanian devil pups are supposed to do.

Because the pups were getting older, Mum often
let them play outside the den. But soon after the sun
rose, the family would go inside, curl up together,
and sleep away the heat of the day.

They were a very happy Tasmanian devil family.

But one night, Mum did not come home. The pups waited quietly at the back of the den as the moon went up and the moon went down. They waited quietly at the front of the den as the sun crossed the sky. And by the time the day grew old, the pups were peeking their heads outside.

Big Stanley did not want to wait anymore. He stomped out of the den, looked back at his mates, and then stomped down the hill.

Soon afterward, Burnie crawled out of the den, sniffed the air, and sneaked his way down the hill.

Finally, Winnie stepped out, turned her head
sideways for a listen, and then ran down the hill.

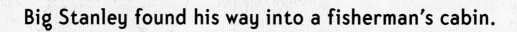
Big Stanley found his way into a fisherman's cabin.

He liked the goodies that he found in the garbage can. He liked the box of noodles that he found on the table. But he did not like the fisherman who came home and tried to catch him.

Big Stanley bashed his way through the things on the table and ran out the door, looking for a place to hide.

Burnie ran up and down the rocks on the beach.
He jumped at the sea foam. He found an old fish
to eat. But as soon as he turned his back on the
ocean, a big wave crashed down on him.

Burnie pulled himself out of the water and
skittered down the shoreline, looking for
a place to hide.

Winnie followed some loud crunching noises until she found a gnarly old devil having a feast. Winnie was hungry, too. But as soon as she lifted a paw to go near, the old devil bared his teeth and screamed, "Argh!"

Winnie scurried down the beach, looking for a place to hide.

Winnie found Burnie—who had found Big Stanley—and they all hid in a big driftwood log. Burnie was scared of all the animals moving around outside. But Winnie remembered how the gnarly old devil had scared her away.

She stuck her head out of the log and screamed, "Argh!" and some wallabies ran away.

"Argh!" Big Stanley tried screaming, too, and a wombat waddled away.

"Argh!" Burnie screamed, and an echidna shuffled away.

Suddenly all three pups stopped.

"Arrrrgh!"

From up on the rocks came another scream.

"Arrrrgh!"

It was Mum.

The three Tasmanian devil pups jumped out of the log.

They raced across the foreshore,

Splashed through the water,

scrambled up the rocks.

At the top they found Mum caught in a trap.

Next to it stood the gnarly old devil who had scared Winnie the night before. When he growled, the pups backed up. When he screamed, they backed up again.

Then Winnie stopped. He was a mean old devil. But they had to save their mum!

"Argh!" screamed Winnie.

"Argh!" screamed Big Stanley.

"Aaaarrrggh!" screamed Burnie.

"Argh! Arrgh! Arrrgh!" the three pups screamed together.

One pup screaming alone was one thing, but three pups screaming together was two pups too much.

The gnarly old devil snarled
and slinked away.

Mum didn't mind when Big Stanley chewed on the stake that held the trap to the ground. She didn't mind when Burnie and Winnie tried to tear the trap apart.

Mum didn't mind when she was tossed upside down and banged around as the pups tried to get her out of the cage. Mum didn't care that they acted gnarly and rough.

Because that is what Tasmanian devils are supposed to do.

Mum was dizzy. The trapdoor
was dented and loose. But still one
stubborn bar held the door shut.

Suddenly Burnie and Winnie ran behind a rock.
Big Stanley lowered his head, gave the trap one big
bash—and knocked it right off the outcropping.

The trap spun through the air like a footy ball at the Grand Final game. And as soon as the trap turned on end, the stubborn bar fell loose and the door came open.

Mum was free of the cage before it hit the
water below.

Burnie and Winnie and Big Stanley ran to their mum. They were a happy family once again.

## Author's Note

While living in Australia, I asked my readers what kind of marsupial they would like me to create a book about. The Tasmanian devil won the vote. I traveled to the only place where they exist in the wild, an Australian island called Tasmania. A man named Geoff King allowed me to move into a fishing shack on his land, located on a stretch of rugged beach in an area called Marrawah.

Wind howled constantly as wallabies, wombats, and echidnas prowled the landscape. And each night at dusk, frightening screams announced the arrival of the Tasmanian devils. I watched them carefully as I drew them in my sketchbook. By observing them over several weeks, I began to appreciate their personalities and patterns. I grew to like the feisty animals.

Tasmanian devils will eat almost anything. They also like to "borrow" things from homes (and fishing cabins) and take them back to their dens. Though fearsome tales have been told about the animal, I found them to be rather timid toward man. But the species is in trouble. A terrible ailment called devil facial tumor disease threatens to make the entire wild population extinct.

I would like to thank the many Tasmanian people who helped me research this story, including Geoff King, Nick Mooney, Jude Lennox, Angela Pinfold, and Jenny Banks.

The three Tasmanian devil pups in this story were named after the nearby Tasmanian towns of Burnie, Wynyard, and Stanley.

# Australia

Sydney

Canberra ★

Melbourne

Marrawah

# Tasmania

*To Geoff King and Nick Mooney*

P A T R I C I A   L E E   G A U C H ,   E D I T O R

**PHILOMEL BOOKS**
A division of Penguin Young Readers Group.
Published by The Penguin Group.

Penguin Group (USA) Inc., 375 Hudson Street, New York, NY 10014, U.S.A.

Penguin Group (Canada), 90 Eglinton Avenue East, Suite 700, Toronto, Ontario M4P 2Y3, Canada (a division of
Pearson Penguin Canada Inc.).

Penguin Books Ltd, 80 Strand, London WC2R 0RL, England.

Penguin Ireland, 25 St. Stephen's Green, Dublin 2, Ireland (a division of Penguin Books Ltd).

Penguin Group (Australia), 250 Camberwell Road, Camberwell, Victoria 3124, Australia
(a division of Pearson Australia Group Pty Ltd).

Penguin Books India Pvt Ltd, 11 Community Centre, Panchsheel Park,
New Delhi - 110 017, India.

Penguin Group (NZ), 67 Apollo Drive, Rosedale, North Shore 0632,
New Zealand (a division of Pearson New Zealand Ltd).

Penguin Books (South Africa) (Pty) Ltd, 24 Sturdee Avenue, Rosebank,
Johannesburg 2196, South Africa.

Penguin Books Ltd, Registered Offices: 80 Strand, London WC2R 0RL, England.

Design by Semadar Megged.   Text set in Caslon 3.
The paintings for this story were created with oil paint on stretched canvas.

Library of Congress Cataloging-in-Publication Data
Blake, Robert J.   Little devils / Robert J. Blake.   p. cm.   Summary: When their mother fails to return one night,
three Tasmanian devil cubs venture out of their den in search of food and, by doing what Tasmanian devils are
supposed to do, manage to save their mother from a trap.   1. Tasmanian devil—Juvenile fiction. [1. Tasmanian
devil—Fiction. 2. Mother and child—Fiction. 3. Tasmania—Fiction.] I. Title.   PZ10.3.B5815Lit 2009
[E]—dc22   2008048106
ISBN 978-0-399-24322-6
1 3 5 7 9 10 8 6 4 2